To Q, R, C, and my very own
E, you inspire me daily.

Thank you!

www.mascotbooks.com

Franny the Nanny in Gumdrops for Breakfast

For more information, please contact:
Mascot Books
620 Herndon Parkway #320
Herndon, VA 20170
info@mascotbooks.com

Library of Congress Control Number: 2017910184

CPSIA Code: PRT1017A
ISBN-13: 978-1-68401-397-5

Printed in the United States

Franny the Nanny in Gumdrops for Breakfast

Written by
Sarah King

Illustrated by
Morgan Ritchie

"I want candy!" Caleb shrieked.

"I want cake!" Alan shouted.

"I want donuts!" Febe hollered.

That is all us kids ever demanded.
Who wants apples, spinach,
chicken, or whole grains? Yuck!
Sweet yummy sugary treats are
what we want to eat.

"What a fantastical morning we have before us, kiddies," said Franny the Nanny. "Who wants grainy granola with Greek yogurt all the way from Greece? "

"Greece? **Gross!**" the kids said in unison.

"Are you trying to make us **sick?**" Febe asked.

"On the contrary, my sweet petunia," Franny said.

"Little kiddies, if you don't eat healthy food, how will you grow up to compete in the Olympics and win gold medals in every event? How will you win the Nobel Peace Prize or discover the newest, brainiest super food? Just because it's green, doesn't mean it won't taste **yummy**."

We didn't hear anything Franny said. We whined and whined and whined, until...something SNAPPED.

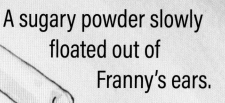

A sugary powder slowly floated out of Franny's ears.

Her eyes began to **glisten** like shiny chocolate-frosted cupcakes. And her hair...it turned into squiggly red licorice! A sweet candy perfume suddenly scented the air.

"**Righty-o** children, how about cereal?" Franny inquired. "We have gummy gumdrops swimming in chocolate milk. Or donuts smothered in frosting, topped with rainbow sprinkles and powdered sugar. To drink, we have apple juice made with 100% sugar and artificial apple flavoring."

CHOCOLATE MILK

ARTIFICI

100%

"Who needs granola and real fruit?!"

"What happened to Franny?" Febe asked under her breath. This was all **fishy**, but we didn't dare ask any questions. Franny spent the rest of the morning in the kitchen, clouds of powdered sugar puffing this way and that.

For lunch, we had a mound of cinnamon toast sandwiches with **ooey-gooey** marshmallow spread and **deep-fried** pound cake French fries with **silky** caramel dipping sauce.

To wash it all down, we had vanilla milkshakes with whipped cream and cherries on top. Everything was delicious!

We couldn't wait for dinner, our next stop on this sugarcapade. Time passed slower than taffy stretching.

By dinner time, Franny the Nanny was permanently surrounded by a cloud of powdered sugar. The avalanche of sugar was starting to change our Franny, but we were bouncing off the walls!

Our eyes **shimmered** like sugar clouds as Franny set before us a huge bowl of licorice spaghetti. It was swimming in strawberry jam sauce with a heavy dusting of powdered sugar. **Delicious!**

Once our sugar rush wore off, it was time for bed. That night, we dreamed of dancing gumdrops and cupcakes in cotton candy tutus.

By day four of the sugar overload,
Franny had transformed even more...

Each day she drowned in sweetness. Each tablespoon of sugar she cooked with made her more **frantic, frenzied,** and **frankly berserk!** Her hair was a bushy mess of electric, red, snake-like licorice ropes. A trail of fluffy powdered sugar footprints followed Franny everywhere. Her chocolate glazed lipstick was smeared all over her face in a clown smile. Franny looked like a **crazy sugar lady**, but something was wrong with us too. We were beginning to look like green, slimy, sticky, slow-moving slugs.

"It's a warm sunny day out there. Get off those rears and get outside," bellowed Franny from the sugar cave we once called the kitchen. Now it just looked like someone had vomited every sweet ever invented all over the place.

"Alrighty!" declared Franny. "Perhaps a breakfast of brown sugar waffles drenched in syrup, whipped cream, and, of course, powdered sugar will pull you three out of this low down hum drum slum drum. Where's the excitement, dumplings?"

Our faces were pale. Our eyes, sunken in.

"I don't feel good," Febe moaned.

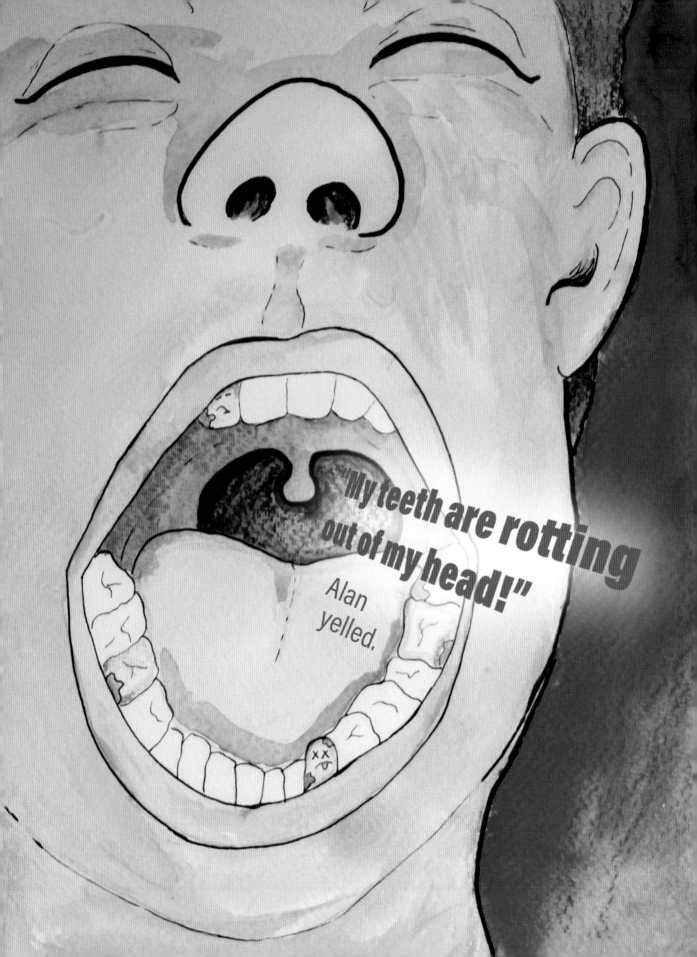

"**NO MORE SUGAR!** We can't take it anymore!" Caleb shrieked. "Last night I had a dream a giant cake monster was attacking me. He made me eat pounds and pounds of sugar until I exploded into a powdery dust."

Alan chimed in, "And your perfume!"

"Yes?" questioned Franny.

"It STINKS!" we all screamed.

"You smell so sweet we want to puke," Alan added.

"No more sugar?"
Franny asked calmly.

"No more. We want healthy food, Franny,"
Caleb pleaded. "We want protein-packed
veggie omelets, bananas, and whole-grain
toast. And milk. Plain, old, white milk.
Our muscles miss protein."

"We don't want powdered sugar on top of everything anymore," Alan said. "We're **sugared-out!**"

"Please, Franny. No more sugar," Febe begged.

Franny the Nanny had a sly smile, "I must say I'm a little shocked. But I'll be happy to make healthy meals. We'll stick with the healthiest of the healthy foods and, of course, no dessert."

The three of us looked at each other...

"**Wait a second,**" Caleb said, "we didn't say no dessert ever. We want sugar, just not that much. We'll have our greens and beans first, **please!**"

About the *Author*

Sarah has been both a nanny and a writer since 2008. After college, she started nannying for a family with one boy. Before long, the family grew with two more babies arriving, which sucked Sarah in even deeper. But this was a wonderful thing, as it inspired Sarah's writings and her creation of Franny the Nanny! *Gumdrops for Breakfast* is Sarah's first published children's book.

Sarah lives in Cary, North Carolina, with her husband, son, dog, and two cats. She would like to give special thanks not only to her boys, but to her family who has supported her unconditionally.

Instagram: sarah.s.king

www.sarahsking.com

About the
Illustrator

Morgan Ritchie has had a passion for illustration from a very early age. She studied Art and Design at North Carolina State University and has maintained a hand in art since. Traditional materials with modern application are of particular interest and influence to her style. Morgan previously worked as a studio assistant for a successful artist and then focused on travel. She currently lives in Cyprus with her husband and daughter.